LILY
OF THE
FOREST

BY BRIAN McCONNACHIE
ILLUSTRATED BY JACK ZIEGLER

CROWN PUBLISHERS, INC., NEW YORK

To Mary

E

McC

Text copyright © 1987 by Brian McConnachie
Illustrations copyright © 1987 by Jack Ziegler
All rights reserved. No part of this book may be reproduced or transmitted in any form or by
any means, electronic or mechanical, including photocopying, recording, or by any informa-
tion storage and retrieval system, without permission in writing from the publisher.
Published by Crown Publishers, Inc. 225 Park Avenue South, New York, New York 10003 and
represented in Canada by the CANADIAN MANDA GROUP.
Crown is a trademark of Crown Publishers, Inc.
Manufactured in Japan
Library of Congress Cataloging-in-Publication Data. McConnachie, Brian. Lily of the forest.
Summary: When a bored young girl becomes lost in the forest, several animals come to her
rescue. [1. Boredom—Fiction. 2. Lost children—Fiction. 3. Forest animals—Fiction] I. Ziegler,
Jack, ill. II. Title.
PZ7.M4784142Li 1987   [E]   87-460
ISBN 0-517-56595-1

10 9 8 7 6 5 4 3 2 1

First Edition

The village of Dun Gannon Gil Gook sat peacefully on the banks of the River Voo and that was the only peaceful thing about the place. It was a busy, busy town.

Everyone there worked all day and every day making dog houses. They worried that somewhere else there was *another* town making dog houses, and this made them work even harder and faster.

One day, a young girl named Lily, who painted smiles on the doggie faces, got sick and tired of her job.

"I don't want to do this anymore," she said to her parents. "It's boring and I'm bored!"

"You're what???!!!" came their amazed reply.

Well, with that her father led her out of the village, across the bridge, and …

sat her down on the ground by a tree.

"You're bored, are you? Well, you just sit here with nothing to do and let's see how you like that!" And he returned to the village.

Lily had never been in these woods before. In fact, she had never been out of the village.

She couldn't sit still.
It was a warm autumn day.

The breezes were blowing,
the birds were singing...so deeper and
deeper she wandered into the woods.

But as the day wore on, its light began to fade
and the night began to grow and everything
stopped being so wonderful.

The less she could see, the more she could hear. And the more she could hear, the worse it sounded. Horrible beasts were everywhere. She huddled into a ball and trembled all night.

The dawn finally came and it brought
another day as beautiful as the one before.
But Lily was lost, so she decided to build a
little shelter in case she had to spend another
night in the forest.

Some animals stopped to watch and
asked what she was doing. Lily told them, and
much to her surprise, they all wanted to help.

Some of the animals had terrific suggestions.

The birds said, "Build your home in a tree and make most of it round."

The rabbits said, "Have lots of rooms and have secret passages connecting them all."

The beavers said, "Why not have a big slide that goes right from your bed into the pond?"

And the place grew bigger and more amazing by the day.

In the evening, the animals gathered around and Lily told them about the humans—how they would brush their teeth, and wear underwear, and read from books. The animals came from all over the forest to hear her. They loved her stories.

But back in the village, Lily's parents were very upset. They couldn't find her anywhere.

They searched and searched and called her name but she was nowhere to be found.

Finally, they started asking the animals. "Have you seen a bored little girl about this high?"

"The only girl we know," the animals answered, "is the enchanted princess who lives in the forest palace. Maybe she can help you."

They didn't want an enchanted princess, they wanted their Lily.

So on and on they searched.

Other animals came forth and suggested, "If you have human troubles you must consult with the all-wise enchanted princess of the forest palace."

And that's what they finally decided to do.

So they traveled this way.

Then they made a mistake and had to go back that way.

Until finally...

There it was! The forest palace! They knew whoever lived there must be strong and wise and mighty.

Would the enchanted princess help them find their Lily?

As they waited they grew more and more nervous. So nervous, in fact, that they didn't recognize their own little girl when she came out to greet them.

"Please, Your Majesty, in all your great wisdom, tell us where we can find our little girl. We miss her so and want to hold her in our arms again. We're sorry for what we did."

"Hey, Mom and Dad!" Lily cried. "It's me, your lovely daughter!"

They could barely believe it. They jumped in
the air with happiness.

Soon, her mom and dad said, "Let's go home."

But Lily replied, "I have a better idea. Let's stay here."

Mom and Dad thought for a moment; maybe that *was* a better idea.

Lily promised they would never run out of
wonderful things to do.

But if they did, and they grew bored, they
could always start making dog houses again.